LOWRIDERS
BLAST from the PAST

By
CATHY CAMPER

Illustrated by
RAÚL THE THIRD

chronicle books · san francisco

WHAT DO YOU NEED TO FORM A LOWRIDER CAR CLUB THAT WILL CHANGE THE WORLD?

IT BEGAN WITH A FRIENDSHIP THAT UNITED THE FLEXIBLE SKILLS OF FLAPJACK OCTOPUS, THE MECHANICAL FINESSE OF LUPE IMPALA, AND MOSQUITO ELIRIO MALARIA'S PASSION FOR PAINTING WORDS.

ONE DAY MANY YEARS AGO, ELIRIO WAS JUST A NIÑO,* FARTING AROUND WITH HIS BROTHERS . . .

BRRM, BRRM, all props are go!

BRAP!!

* KID

* MY SONS! ** DAD, WE MISSED YOU! *** YOUR GIFTS, MY SONS

* WORDS

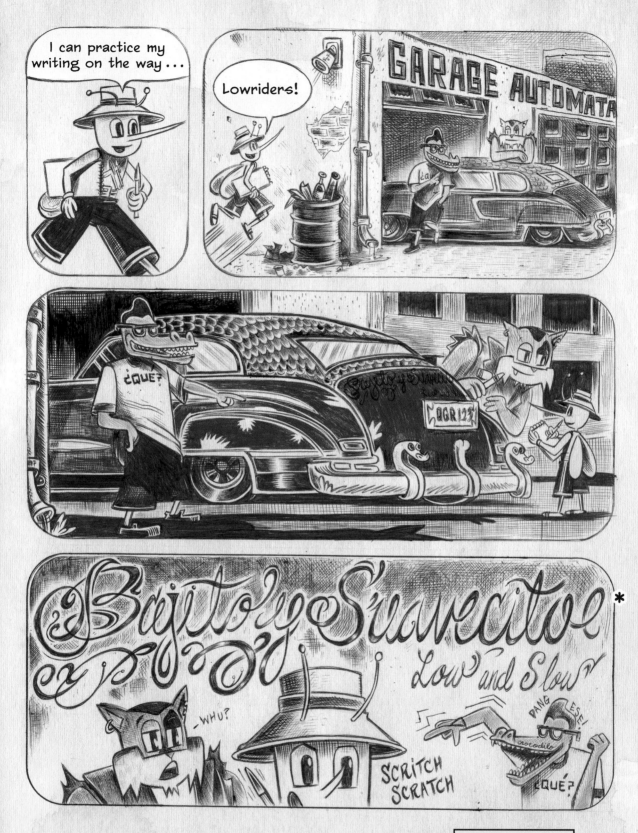

* LOW AND SLOW

* MURALS; PAINTINGS DONE ON WALLS ** SEE YOU LATER, SIRS!

* HAMBURGER ** BACON *** STUPID

* HI ** MOM

* HOUSE OF THE SEA ** MY HEART *** A POPULAR MEXICAN TV COMEDY SHOW FOR KIDS

* STOP!

* OCTOPUS

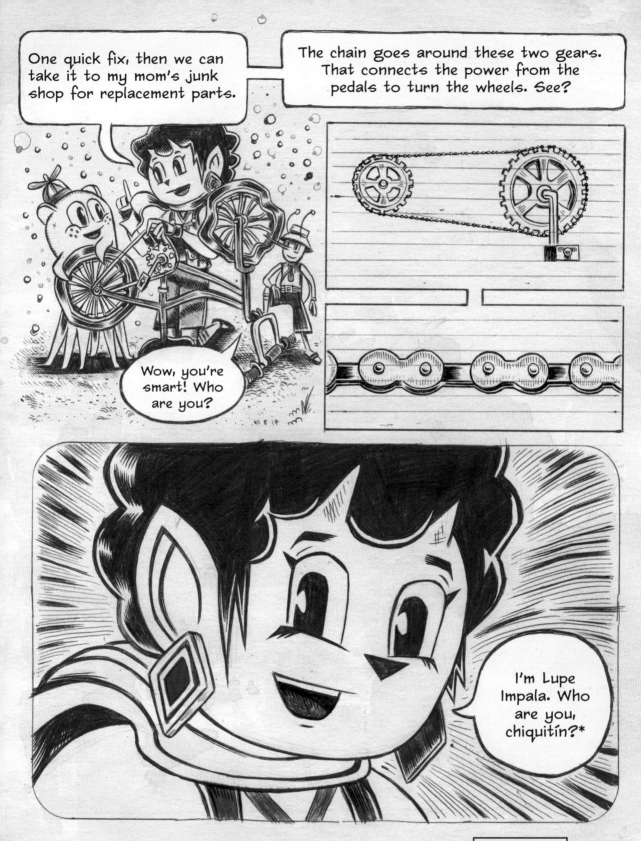

I'm El Chavo Flapjack Octopus del Mar. Junior.

But you can just call me El Chavo.

Or Flappy.

That's my mom, Angélica! And my dad plays the guitarrón**** for Los Mariscos!

THUNK

Ay chihuahua,* you got enough names for both of us!

Are you related to the mariachi** band Angélica del Mar y Los Mariscos?***

Wow! They play at all the fiestas.***** I know because my Mamá Gazelle makes all the decorations.

LOS MARISCOS

* AN EXPRESSION OF DISBELIEF   ** A SMALL, STROLLING BAND THAT PERFORMS MEXICAN FOLK MUSIC   *** ANGÉLICA OF THE OCEAN AND THE SEAFOOD   **** MARIACHI GUITAR   ***** PARTIES

* MY NAME IS ** ARTIST *** YES

* COME ON!

THAT'S HARRY GAMBOA JUNIOR. IN HIGH SCHOOL, HE ORGANIZED PROTESTS AGAINST BAD CONDITIONS IN POOR SCHOOLS.

YA ¡BASTA!

RAZA SI! GUERRA No!

INVEST IN TOMORROW

EDUCATE TODAY!

CHICANO POWER

HUELGA

FAIR CHANCE

EDUCA NO CONT

THERE'S HIS PAL WILLIE HERRÓN. WHEN HIS BROTHER GOT BEATEN UP, HE MADE A MURAL ABOUT IT THAT USED GRAFFITI ALREADY ON THE WALL.

VEX

ARTIST WILLIE HERRON →

AZTLAN FRAW

AND GRONK LIKED TO HANG OUT AT LIBRARIES AND DRAW, PROBABLY LIKE YOU, ELIRIO. WHEN HE WAS A KID, HE MADE CLAY MASKS AND BURIED THEM ALL OVER EAST L.A. SO FUTURE ARCHAEOLOGISTS WOULD FIND THEM.

AND PATSSI VALDEZ! SHE DRESSED UP FOR ASCO AS THE UNIVERSE—SHE WAS A WALKING MURAL, INSTEAD OF A PAINTED ONE!

They have a lowrider?

Yes, and they're applying today. We could go with them!

Only cars that meet certain standards get accepted. And if you get in, people come from all around to look at all the cars and how cool they are! It's a major deal to get accepted. I hope we do.

I can't wait to see all those carros!*

MEW

MEW

MEW

¿Qué es eso?**

MEW

42

* CARS ** WHAT'S THAT?

* HOW COOL! ** HOW STUCK UP!

My Mamá Impala runs the junk store, over here.

My Mamá Gazelle runs her workshop, over there . . . ¡Vamos! I'll show you . . .

This is Mamá Impala. Hi, Mamá! These are my friends, El Chavo and Elirio.

Nice to meet you!

Here's my work space. Usually I fix small things, but someday I want to work on cars!

"ALL THIS IS FOR SALE, BUT I CAN PICK THROUGH IT FOR MY PROJECTS . . ."

And right through that door is Mamá Gazelle's workshop . . .

Ooohhh!

¡Pájaros carpinteros!*

¡Papel picado!**

Shhh! It's our secret.

Eh, chiquito,*** you must be one of Lupita's amigos,**** no? Promise to keep our woodpecker studio a secret.

OK.

"THEY'RE VERY RARE IVORY-BILLED WOODPECKERS. THEY HAVEN'T BEEN SEEN IN THE U.S. FOR DECADES."

IVORY-BILLED Woodpecker

"PEOPLE HAVE BEEN SEARCHING FOR THESE BIRDS FOR YEARS. THEY THINK THE BIRDS MIGHT BE EXTINCT, AND HAVE EVEN OFFERED PRIZE MONEY TO FIND ONE. THE BIRDS COME HERE TO MAKE ART, AND TO HIDE."

Promise not to tell?

We promise!

* WOODPECKERS! ** LACY DESIGNS CUT FROM COLORED TISSUE PAPER TO USE AS DECORATIVE BANNERS *** KID **** FRIENDS

53

* MONEY

* LITTLE THORNS ** THE BEAUTIFUL ROSES

* THESE JERKS ARE SUCH A PAIN! ** A MACHO GUY

* HAIR

* GUYS, DUDES

* MY SON

* WHAT'S GOING ON? ** MY LOVE *** MY NEW FRIENDS

* ALL RIGHT, RIGHT ON

* HOW BEAUTIFUL! ** NEW PAINT *** WHITE

* NUMBER ONE ** NO GOOD

* NUMBER TWO

* BOSS'S SIGNATURE ** THE BOSS

* CHICKEN

* LOSERS!

* BUZZARD

* TURKEY

* RIGHT, OF COURSE! ** HOW STRONG!

* WATERMELON

WHAT DOES IT MEAN / ¿QUE SIGNIFICA?

¿A dónde vas?—Where are you going?

adiós—goodbye

agua fresca—("fresh water") cold, fruity drink that may also contain flowers or seeds

aguacate—avocado

amigos—friends

Angélica del Mar y los Mariscos—Angélica of the Ocean and Seafood

artista—artist

Ay chihuahua, Aye yi yi—expressions of disbelief

bajito y suavecito—low and slow

beícon—bacon

bichito—little insect

blanco—white

buena suerte—good luck

cacahuate—peanut

carro, carros—car, cars

casa del mar—house of the sea

chica, chicas—girl, girls

chido—cool

chiquitín—little one

chiquito—kid

churros—strips of fried sweet dough, like a doughnut

claro—right, of course

compressor—a machine that increases the pressure of air or gas

cuate—buddy

de voladita—in a snap, right away

dinero—money

El Chavo—literally, "the boy," but also referring to *El Chavo del Ocho*, a popular Mexican TV comedy show for kids

el famoso muralista—the famous muralist

el jefe—the boss

Entren a mi telearaña—Come into my spiderweb

ese—dude

espinitas—little thorns

estrellas—stars

estúpido—stupid

exacto—exactly

fiestas—parties

firma del jefe—boss's signature

fuchi—pew

gracias—thank you

guajolote—turkey

guitarrón—big bass mariachi guitar

hamburguesa—hamburger

¡Hasta luego, señores!—See you later, sirs!

hola—hi

homie—short for homeboy, something you'd call a friend or someone you know

¡Huele a puro chivo aquí!—It smells like pure goats in here!

huevos fritos—fried eggs

increíble— incredible, amazing

insecto—insect

invertebrate—an animal without a backbone, like an octopus, clam, crab, or insect. This word is the same in Spanish and English.

ivory-billed woodpecker—a large woodpecker with a thirty-inch wingspan, probably extinct, whose habitat was the southeastern United States and Cuba.

ja ja—ha ha

ji ji ji—hee hee hee

Las Rosas Hermosas—the Beautiful Roses

llantas—tires

Lo siento—I'm sorry

Los Matamoscas—the Flyswatters

mamá—mom

mariachi—a small, strolling band that performs Mexican folk music

más gigante—much bigger

me gusta—I like

me llamo—my name is

mi amor—my love

mi corazón—my heart

mi'jo—my son

mi mamá—my mom

mis nuevos amigos—my new friends

mis hijos—my sons

mis murales—my murals

muchas gracias—many thanks

mujer, mujeres—woman, women

¡Mujeres, tenían queser!—It had to be women, of course!

murales—murals; paintings done on walls

niño, niños—kid, kids

¿Niños, qué pasa aquí?—Kids, what is going on in there?

no bueno—no good

número uno—number one

número dos—number two

ocelote—ocelot

Órale—All right, Right on

pájaros carpinteros—woodpeckers

palabras—words

palabras estúpidas—stupid words

Papá—dad

¡Papá, te extrañamos!—Dad, we missed you!

papel picado—lacy designs cut from colored tissue paper to use as decorative banners

PÁRATE—STOP

pedos—farts

pelo—hair

perdedores—losers

pintura nueva—new paint

pollo—chicken

¿Por qué no?—Why not?

pulpo—octopus

¡Qué bonito!—How beautiful!

¡Qué chido!—How cool!

¿Qué es eso?—What's that?

¡Qué fuerte!—How strong!

¿Qué hacen aquí?—What are you doing here?

¿Qué pasa?—What's going on?

¿Qué pasa, escuincle?—What's happening, pipsqueak?

¡Qué pesados estos tipos!—These jerks are such a pain!

¡Qué sangrón!—How conceited, stuck up!

¿Qué te pasó?—What happened to you?

sandía—watermelon

señor, señores—mister, sirs

sí—yes

Sí, amorcito, dame un beso—Yes, little love, give me a kiss

¡Soy el Hindenburg!—I'm the Hindenburg!

súbanse—climb in, get up

Sus regalos, mis hijos—Your gifts, my sons

tatuaje—tattoo

un gatito—a kitten

un macho—a macho guy

una campanita—a little bell

vamos—come on

vámonos—let's go

vatos—guys, dudes

watcha—look

zapatos—shoes

zopilote—buzzard

Character development
sketches by Raúl the Third.

AUTHOR'S NOTES

Indigenous Words

When Western European countries colonized the Americas, their languages of English and Spanish (and also French, Dutch, and Portuguese) also took over. Colonialists prevented Indigenous people from speaking their own languages, forced Western culture on Indigenous people through missions and boarding schools, and smothered Indigenous culture that incorporated language, such as religion and music. Spanish and English became the "official" languages of the Americas, and yet, within these languages, many words from Indigenous American languages managed to survive. These embedded Indigenous words are also called "loanwords."

American Indigenous words come from many different groups of people and from many different eras. Many Indigenous languages still exist and thrive; Nahuatl, the language of the Aztecs, has been spoken for centuries, and the Nahua peoples of Mexico still speak variants of it today.

Sadly, colonialism also led to the extinction of many Indigenous languages. Indigenous peoples have fought back to keep their languages alive. They've offered language classes aimed particularly at young people; created books, art, and media in their languages; and represented their cultures as living cultures, not ones lost to history.

Some Indigenous words, like coyote and squash, were adopted into English and Spanish because the Europeans had no words to describe these things that were new to them. Many other Indigenous words remain as names and descriptions for places and geographic features. For example, the Miami-Illinois word shikaakwa, which means "striped skunk" or "smelly onion or weeds," became Chicago, its pronunciation altered a bit by the French explorers. Chapultepec means "a hill of grasshoppers," combining the Nahuatl words tepec, meaning "on a hill," and chapulines, meaning "grasshoppers." Understanding what Indigenous words mean tells us more about the people, land, places, things, and history of the Americas.

Jack Weatherford's books, *Indian Givers: How the Indians of the Americas Transformed the World* and *Native Roots: How the Indians Enriched America*, discuss Indigenous inventions and language absorbed by present-day American culture. The Native Roots chapter, "The Naming of North America," is an insightful look at Indigenous place names and language in the United States.

Other books on this topic include *O Brave New Words! Native American Loanwords in Current English* by Charles Cutler and *Everything You Wanted to Know About Indians and Were Afraid to Ask* by Anton Treuer. The children's book *A Native American Thought of It: Amazing Inventions and Innovations* by Rocky Landon with David MacDonald also has a short section on Indigenous words that have been added to English.

Here are some familiar loanwords in English and Spanish (some of which are used in this book) that you might know, listed under their original Indigenous languages, as best can be determined.

Arawak and Carib
iguana

Arawak (Taino)
guava
hammock
hurricane
potato
yucca

Carib
canoe

French-Canadian adaptation from Micmac, Abenaki
toboggan

French-Canadian adaptation from Ojibwa
muskellunge

Guugu Yimidhirr (Australia)
kangaroo

Inuit
igloo
kayak

Micmac (Algonquian)
caribou

Nahuatl
aguacate (Sp.)—avocado
cacahuate (Sp.)—peanut
chia
chili
cocoa
coyote
guacamole
jalapeño
mesquite
nopal
peyote
tamale
tequila
tomato

Sami
tundra

Tupi
buccaneer
capybara
cashew
cayenne
cougar
ipecac
jaguar
piranha
tapioca
toucan

Ivory-Billed Woodpeckers

In the nineteenth century, the ivory-billed woodpecker lived throughout the southern United States, including Florida, and Cuba. Habitat destruction and hunting drove it to extinction status. But no one knows for sure if the bird is totally gone. Many videos, photos, and sound recordings claim to offer evidence of sightings, but none of these have truly documented that ivory-bills still exist.

In 2006 an anonymous source offered a reward of $10,000 for substantive evidence of the bird's existence in Arkansas, but so far, no one has conclusive proof of a living bird, as no confirmed sightings have occurred since the 1940s.

Artists

Harry Gamboa Jr., Gronk, Willie Herrón, and Patssi Valdez were members of an East Los Angeles art collective called Asco (Spanish for disgust or nausea), who did activist performance art. In 1972, frustrated by what they saw as the racism and lack of Mexican American art in the Los Angeles County Museum of Art, Gamboa, Gronk, and Herrón spray-painted their names on the outside of the museum, claiming the whole museum (which would not exhibit their work) as their work of art. The next day they documented their conceptual work with a photograph of Patssi Valdez posing near their signatures.

How an Airbrush Works and the Venturi Effect

The airbrush was patented in 1876 by Francis Edgar Stanley, one of the twin brothers who invented the Stanley Steamer automobile. An airbrush paints with a fine mist of paint; it can create subtle, atomized mixes of colors.

When you press the trigger of an airbrush, air flows through the inner tube of the airbrush and comes out the nozzle. A needle in the airbrush controls the quality of the paint. At first, no paint comes out, but as you pull the trigger back farther, the airbrush needle withdraws, allowing a ring of space around the needle through which the atomized paint flows. The Venturi Effect creates the suction, which draws up the paint.

The Venturi Effect is named for physicist Giovanni Battista Venturi. It describes how the velocity (speed) of a fluid increases as it flows through a pinched or narrowed section of pipe, while the fluid pressure is reduced, creating suction. This spray effect is similar to the jet effect that happens when you put your thumb over the nozzle of a garden hose; the water squirts further because the hose opening has been made smaller by your thumb.

The Venturi Effect is used when air needs to be mixed with another ingredient, since the suction pulls the secondary ingredient into the air. Airbrushes mix air and paint; Bunsen burners, gas stoves, and grills mix air and gas; and sandblasters mix fine sand with air. It also explains those big gusts of wind you feel in cities. These are formed when wind flows through narrow gaps between tall buildings, which channel and speed up the wind into huge gusts.

Many lowrider artists wanted to paint with airbrushes, but had little access to expensive cans of compressed air or air compressors. Like Lupe and Elirio, some used tires for their air source, refilling the tires multiple times a day. I included this detail in our book to honor and recognize the inventive technology of lowrider culture.

Papel picado

Papel picado means perforated paper (literally translated, it means "pecked paper"). Papel picado are lacy tissue paper decorations for holidays like Easter, Christmas, and Día de los Muertos, as well as weddings, quinceañeras, and other family holidays. The paper cutouts featuring pictures of birds, flowers, skeletons, words, and other designs are ephemeral; they aren't meant to last.

Before Europeans came to the Americas, Aztecs made decorations honoring their gods and goddesses from the bark of fig and mulberry trees. This bark paper was called amatl or amate paper. The Aztec codices were also drawn on this paper. The Spanish banned these Indigenous papers as a way to suppress Indigenous religion and replace it with Catholicism.

The Spanish brought paper and paper-cutting techniques with them. Trade between China and the Americas introduced very thin Chinese tissue paper (called papel chino or papel chinato) that could be cut into lacy patterns.

Originally, papel picado was made by artists following a template, or pattern, cutting many layers of tissue paper at a time using variously sized metal chisels. Today papel picado is mostly machine made, but artisans still make it by hand to preserve the original craft.

ACKNOWLEDGMENTS

A huge thank you to Carlee Smith, Violeta Garza, Diana Miranda, Josh Rodriguez, Lucy Iraola, Mary Conde, Ana Ruiz Morillo, Delia Palomeque Morales, Debbie Reese, Edna Vazquez, Ovarian Psycos, the Unique Ladies, and Gloria Maria Guadalupe Morán, and Asco. Huge thank-yous, from Cathy and Raúl, to Taylor Norman, Ginee Seo, Neil Egan, and everyone at Chronicle for helping us make such wonderful books, and to our agent, Jennifer Laughran, for believing in us. An especially heartfelt thank you to Lee Francis and Anton Trever for their early support of and help with the book.

In honor of all Indigenous people at Standing Rock, who stood up in 2016 to protect water for all living things.

Thank you to all my friends and family, who believed in and supported this book. —C. C.

Thanks to all of the Latino and Mexican artists who paved the way and helped to show me the importance of my experience. And to El Chuco artists Gaspar and Luis Jimenez who made Mexican Americans and El Paso look cool. Thanks to At The Drive-In and The Mars Volta for showing El Paso kids that we could be rock stars. Y muchisimas gracias to Homies Car Club and Chuco Relic for the hometown support. Special thanks to Elaine Ray for her assistance during crunch time. —R.

SOURCES

Harry Gamboa Jr., Willie Herrón, Patssi Valdez, Gronk
Asco Art Collective - Video
https://www.youtube.com
/watch?v=fSQSekn7Ihg
The Asco Interviews
https://www.youtube.com
/watch?v=iyFViWGU06I
Benavidez, Max. *Gronk*. Los Angeles: UCLA Chicano Studies Research Center Press, 2007. Print.
Chicano Pioneers
www.nytimes.com/2011/08/28/arts/design
/works-by-asco-at-the-los-angeles-museum
.html?_r=0
Patssi Valdez/ASCO, Patssi as the Universe, 1974. http://www.imgrum.org/tag/patssivaldez

Ivory-billed woodpeckers
animals.nationalgeographic.com/animals/birds
/ivory-billed-woodpecker/
www.sibleyguides.com/bird-info
/ivory-billed-woodpecker/
http://www.audubon.org/birds-of-america
/ivory-billed-woodpecker
http://www.birds.cornell.edu/ivory/
www.smithsonianmag.com/science-nature
/ghost-of-a-chance-82491331/?no-ist

Papel picado
www.mexconnect.com/articles/1567-mexico
-s-traditional-papel-picado-classic-art-for-a-
mexican-fiesta

http://www.zocalotx.com/papelpicado.htm
How to Make Papel Picado Using a Template
https://www.youtube.com
/watch?v=Psmc1D2ddQo
How to Make Papel Picado (Spanish)
https://www.youtube.com
/watch?v=-gQlszGKjdU

Indigenous words
Cutler, Charles L. *O Brave New Words!: Native American Loanwords in Current English*. Norman: University of Oklahoma Press, 2000, 1994.
Landon, Rocky, and David MacDonald. *A Native American Thought of It: Amazing Inventions and Innovations*. Toronto: Annick Press, 2008.
Treuer, Anton. *Everything You Wanted to Know About Indians But Were Afraid to Ask*. Saint Paul: Borealis Books, 2012.
Weatherford, Jack. *Indian Givers: How Native Americans Transformed the World*. New York: Three Rivers Press, 1988, 2010.
Weatherford, Jack. *Native Roots: How the Indians Enriched America*. New York: Crown, 1991.
https://www.manataka.org/page263.html
http://www.todayifoundout.com/index
.php/2013/07/how-chicago-got-its-name/
Indian Words in English
http://nativeamericanetroots.net/diary/1223
Oxford Dictionaries: More than Just Moccasins; American Indian Words in English
http://blog.oxforddictionaries.com/2011/11
/american-indian-words-in-english/
Mexico's Place Names and Their Meanings
www.mexconnect.com/articles/3467-mexico
-s-place-names-and-their-meanings

How an Airbrush Works
http://www.air-craft.net/blog/2016/02/08
/how-does-my-airbrush-work/
www.youtube.com/watch?v=baTyyemNkG0
www.youtube.com/watch?v=DNUGr_lNiqs

The Venturi Effect
http://www.tech-faq.com/venturi-effect.html
woodgears.ca/physics/venturi.html
www.bbc.com/news/magazine-33426889

Interview with Rick Munoz: lowrider.
staging.enthusiastnetwork.com/lifestyle/
art/0909-lrap-airbrush-artist-rick-munoz/

DEDICATIONS

To my mom, for her wisdom about bullies, and to Sunny Lozano and his family, and Stefan Lotz and his family—our true fans! **—Cathy Camper**

Big thank you to all of the kids I played and fought with in the apartment complexes of Village Two and Monte Bello on Shadow Mountain. **—Raúl the Third**

Library of Congress Cataloging-in-Publication Data available.

ISBN 978-1-4521-6315-4 [hardcover]
ISBN 978-1-4521-6316-1 [paperback]

Manufactured in China.

Design by Neil J. Egan III.
Typeset in Comiccraft Hedge Backwards, P22 Posada, and ITC Century.

10 9 8 7 6 5 4 3 2 1

Chronicle Books LLC
680 Second Street
San Francisco, California 94107

Chronicle Books—we see things differently. Become part of our community at www.chroniclekids.com.